KU-586-859

THIS WALKER BOOK
BELONGS TO:

. . . .

. . . .

To Ginger,
Oti and Diggy

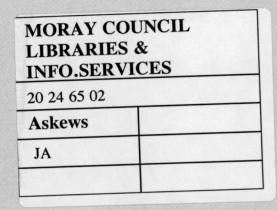

**MORAY COUNCIL
LIBRARIES &
INFO.SERVICES**

20 24 65 02

Askews	
JA	

First published 1997 by Walker Books Ltd
87 Vauxhall Walk, London SE11 5HJ

This edition published 2008

2 4 6 8 10 9 7 5 3 1

© 1997, 2008 Charlotte Voake

The right of Charlotte Voake to be identified
as author/illustrator of this work has been asserted by her in
accordance with the Copyright, Designs and Patents Act 1988

This book has been typeset in Calligraphic.

Printed in China.

All rights reserved. No part of this book may be reproduced, transmitted
or stored in an information retrieval system in any form or by any means, graphic,
electronic or mechanical, including photocopying, taping and recording,
without prior written permission from the publisher.

British Library Cataloguing in Publication Data: a catalogue
record for this book is available from the British Library

ISBN 978-1-4063-1269-0

www.walkerbooks.co.uk

GINGER

Charlotte Voake

WALKER BOOKS

AND SUBSIDIARIES

LONDON • BOSTON • SYDNEY • AUCKLAND

Ginger was a lucky cat.

He lived with
a little girl
who made him
delicious
meals

and gave him
a beautiful basket,

where he would curl up ...

and close
his eyes.

Here he is,
fast asleep.

But here he is again,
WIDE AWAKE.

What's this?

A kitten!

"He'll be a nice new friend for you, Ginger," said the little girl.

But Ginger
didn't want a new friend,
especially one like this.
Ginger hoped the
kitten would
go away,

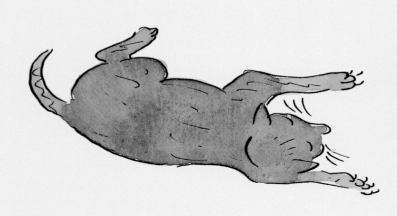

but he didn't.

Everywhere
Ginger went,
the kitten followed,
springing out
from behind
doors,

leaping on to Ginger's back,

even eating
Ginger's food!

What a naughty
kitten!

But what upset Ginger more than anything was that whenever he got into his beautiful basket, the kitten always climbed in too,

and
the little
girl didn't
do anything
about it.

So Ginger decided to leave home.

He went out
through the cat flap
and he didn't come back.

The kitten waited for a bit,
then he got into
Ginger's basket.

It wasn't the same without Ginger.

The kitten
played
with some
flowers,

then he found
somewhere
to sharpen
his claws.

The little girl
found him on the table
drinking some milk.

"You naughty kitten!" she said.

"I thought you were with Ginger. Where is he anyway?"

She looked in Ginger's basket,

but of course he wasn't there.

"Perhaps he's eating his food," she said.

But Ginger wasn't there either.

"I hope he's not upset," she said.

"I hope he hasn't run away."

She put on her wellingtons and went out into the garden, and that is where she found him;

a very wet,
sad, cold Ginger,
hiding under
a bush.

The little girl
carried Ginger
and the kitten
inside.
"It's a pity
you can't
be friends,"
she said.

She gave
Ginger a special meal.

She gave the kitten
a little plate
of his own.

Then she tucked Ginger into his own warm basket.

All she could find for the kitten to sleep in was a little tiny cardboard box.

But the kitten didn't mind, because cats love cardboard boxes (however small they are).

So when the little girl
went in to see
the two cats
again,

THIS is how she found them.

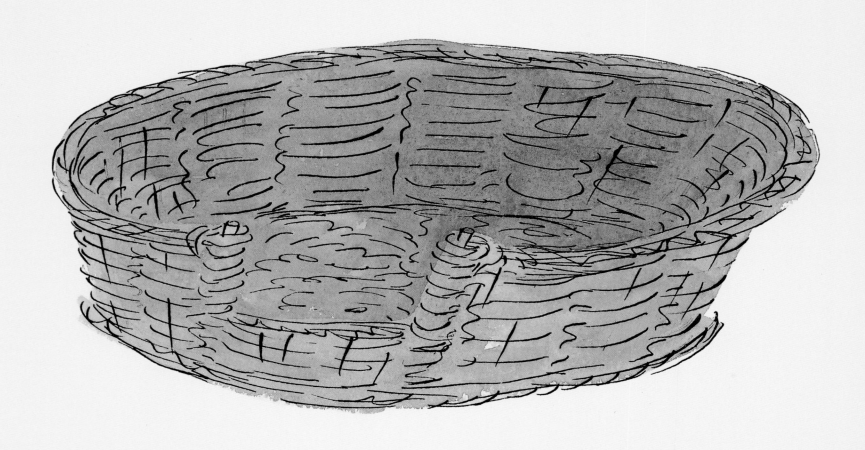

3 8002 02299 586 6

£9.50

CEN **COVENTRY LIBRARIES**

Please return this book on or before
the last date stamped below.

PS130553 Disk 4

Central

1 8 JUN 2018

WITHDRAWN
FOR SALE

To renew this book take it to any of
the City Libraries before
the date due for return

Coventry City Council

لا عَجَلَةَ مَعَ سَلِيمْ!

Not ... ood!

MANTRA
LINGUA

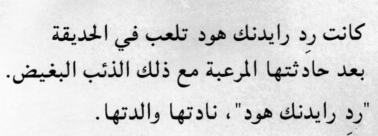

كانت رِد رايدنك هود تلعب في الحديقة
بعد حادثتها المرعبة مع ذلك الذئب البغيض.

"رِد رايدنك هود"، نادتها والدتها.
"لقَد صنعت كوكيز، تعالي وخذي واحدة. ولِمَ لا تأخذي منها لوالدك أيضاً؟"
ولكن رِد رايدنك هود مازالت تشعر بعدم الإطمئنان في الذهاب إلى الغابة.
إلاّ أن والدتها تطلب مساعدتها ووالدها يحب أكل هذه الـ-كوكيز،
لذا وافقت على الذهاب.

Red Riding Hood was playing in the garden after her terrible ordeal
with that nasty wolf.
"Red Riding Hood," called her Mum, "I've made cookies, come and get one.
Why not take some to Dad?"
Now Red Riding Hood still felt a bit nervous about going into the wood. But
Mum needed her help, and Dad loved his cookies. So, she agreed to go.

KU-587-111

Her Mum counted ten freshly made cookies into
a basket. 2, 4, 6, 8, 10.
Red Riding Hood gave her Mum a big
hug and off she went.

وضعت والدتها عشر كوكيز طازجة في السلّة. وعدتها
٢، ٦، ٨، ١٠.
وقبّلت رِد رايدنك هود والدتها وأخذت طريقها إلى الغابة.

ولم تقطع مسافة طويلة حتى سمعت صوتاً ناعماً:
"رد رايدنك هود ، رد رايدنك هود ، هل لديك طعاماً؟"
فقد مضى وقت طويل وأنا في هذه القلعة وأكاد أموت جوعاً.
"إدلِ بسلّتك، لديّ كوكيز طازجة ولذيذة"، قالت رِد رايدنك هود .

She hadn't gone far when she heard a small voice: "Red Riding Hood, Red Riding Hood, have you any food? I've been stuck up in this tower for ages and I'm starving."
"Send down your basket," said Red Riding Hood. "I have a delicious, freshly made cookie for you."

"ما أطيبه، هذا ما
أفضله"، "أنا مسرور
برؤيتك مرة أخرى وبعد وقت
قصير من حادثتك المرعبة مع ذلك
الذئب البغيض"، أجاب رابونزل.

"Yummy, my favourite," replied Rapunzel.
"It's good to see you out again, so soon after
your terrible ordeal with that nasty wolf."

تابعت رد رايدنك هود سيرها مرة ثانية
لتأخذ الَـكوكيز إلى والدها .
نظرت إلى سلّتها فوجدت أن عدد الـكوكيز
قد أصبح ٩ بعد أن كان ١٠!

Red Riding Hood set off again to deliver the
freshly made cookies to her Dad.
She looked into her basket.
10 had become 9!

وبعد فترة وصلت إلى بيت السيّد والسيّدة الدّب. وكانا جالسين حول مائدة الحديقة مع طفلهما الدّب ينظرون إلى ثلاثة صحون فارغة.

"رِد رايدنك هود ، رِد رايدنك هود ، هل لديك طعام؟ نحن نكاد نموت جوعاً. فقد سُرِقت عصيدتنا!"

After a while she arrived at Mr and Mrs Bear's house. They were sitting around their garden table with Baby Bear staring into three very empty bowls.
"Red Riding Hood, Red Riding Hood, have you any food? We're starving. Someone's eaten all our porridge!"

وكانت رد رايدنك هود بنت صغيرة
طيّبة القلَب فوضعت في صحن كل منهم
كوكيز واحدة طازجة.

Now Red Riding Hood was a kind little girl and she popped one freshly
made cookie into each of their bowls.

"أووو شكراً لكِ، نحن مسرورون برؤيتك مرة أخرى، وبعد وقت قصير من حادثتك المرعبة مع ذلك الذئب البغيض"، قال الدّب والدّبة.

"Oooooh, thank you," said the bears. "It's good to see you out again, so soon after your terrible ordeal with that nasty wolf."

وأسرعت رد رايدنك هود في سيرها ، ونظرت في سلّتها.

لقد أَصبح عدد ال-كوكيز ٦ بعد أن كان ٩!

وبعد وقت قصير وصلت إلى بيت جدّتها.

فكرت رِدّ رايدنك هود وقالت لنفسها "يجب أن أطمئن على جدتي بعد حادثتي المرعبة مع ذلك الذئب البغيض".

Red Riding Hood marched on. She looked into her basket.
9 had become 6!
She hadn't gone far when she reached Grandma's house.
"I must see how Grandma is after her terrible ordeal with
that nasty wolf," thought Red Riding Hood.

كانت جدتها في الفراش.
"جدتي، جدتي يبدو عليكِ أنك جوعانة جداً"،
قالت رِد رايدنك هود.

Grandma was in bed.
"Grandma, Grandma, you look starving,"
said Red Riding Hood.

"يجب أن تأخذي واحدة من ال-كوكيز التي صنعتها والدتي. أنا في طريقي لأعطي والدي بعض منها ، ولا أعتقد أنه يمانع في أن تأخذي واحدة منها".

"شكراً يا عزيزتي"، أجابت الجدة. "أنتِ بنت تفكرين في مشاعر الآخرين. والآن أسرعي في طريقك، ولاَ تتركي والدك في الإنتظار طويلاً".

"You must have one of Mum's home made cookies. I'm taking some to Dad, and he won't mind you having one."
"Thank you dear," said Grandma. "You are a thoughtful girl. Now run along and don't keep your father waiting."

وقبّلت رِد رايدنك هود جدتها وأسرعت في الذهاب إلى والدها.
نظرت فَي سلّتها. لقد أصبح عدد الـ-كوكيز ٥ بعد أن كان ٦!

Red Riding Hood gave Grandma a kiss on the cheek
and rushed off to find her Dad.
She looked into her basket. 6 had become 5!

وبعد فترة وصلت إلى النهر. وجدت هناك ثلاثة تيوس ضعيفة الجسم تجلس على بقعة من الحشيش البنّي اليابس.

"رِد رايدنك هود ، رِد رايدنك هود ، هل لديك شيء من الطعام؟ نحن نكاد نموت جوعاً".

After a while she reached the river. Three very scrawny billy goats were lying on a patch of rather brown grass.

"Red Riding Hood, Red Riding Hood, have you any food? We're starving."

"لا نستطيع عبور الجسر لنأكل من الحشيش الأخضر
لأن هناك وحشاً خبيثاً جوعان ينتظر ليأكلنا".

"We can't cross the bridge to eat the lush green grass,"
they said. "There's a mean and hungry
troll waiting to eat us."

"يالكم من مساكين، كُلوا من هذه الـ-كوكيز الطازجة،
إنها لذيذة، ١، ٢، ٣".

"You poor things, try some home made cookies,
they're delicious. 1, 2, 3."

"أنتِ طيبة جداً"، قالت التيوس.
"نحنَ مسرورون برؤيتكِ مرة أخرى بعد
حادثتك المرعبة مع ذلكَ الذئب البغيض".

"You're very kind," said the billy goats. "Nice to see you out again, so soon after your terrible ordeal with that nasty wolf."

أسرعت رِد رايدنك في طريقها. نظرت في سلّتها. لقَد أصبح عدد الـ-كوكيز ٢ عد أن كان ٥!
ثمّ فكرت رد رايدنك هود وقالت لنفسها "على الأقلَ لا يوجد هنا ذئاب بغيضة"، وفي تلك اللحظة...

Red Riding Hood ran on. She looked into her basket. 5 had become 2!
"Well at least there aren't any nasty wolves around here," thought Red Riding Hood.
Just then…

... قفز ذئب أمامها.
"حسناً، حسناً، حسناً!"، قال الذئب. "ليتك لا تكوني رِد رايدنك هود، تخرجين مرة أخرى وبعد وقت قصير من حادثتك المرعبة مع أخي. إن رؤيتك تجعلني أشعر بالجوع".
"لن تأخذ أَيّ واحدة من الـ-كوكيز التي معي"، قالت رِد رايدنك هود بصوت دقيق حاد.

…a wolf jumped out in front of her.
"Well, well, well!" said the wolf. "If it isn't Red Riding Hood out again, so soon after your terrible ordeal with my brother. Seeing you makes me feel rather peckish."
"You can't have any of my cookies," squeaked Red Riding Hood.

"لم أكن أفكر بال-كوكيز"، زمجر الذئب وهو يقفز نحوها.

"I wasn't thinking about cookies,"
growled the wolf as he leapt towards her.

وعند سماعه صراخاً، أسرع والدها حاملاً فأسه بيده.

Hearing a scream, her Dad appeared wielding his axe.

"رِد رايدنك هود! اهربي!"، صاح والدها غاضباً وهو يطرد الذئب بعيداً.
"مرة أخرى، لا، رِد رايدنك هود"، فكر والدها قائلاً لنفسه.

"Run, Red Riding Hood! Run!" he bellowed as he chased the wolf away.
"Not again, Red Riding Hood," thought Dad.

وكانا جائعين بعد هذه الحادثة المرعبة.
والتفتت إلى سلتها وفتّشت عن الـ-كوكيز.
"واحدة لكَ وواحدة لي"، قالت رِد رايدنك هود.

They were both hungry after their terrible ordeal.
She reached into her basket.
"One for you and one for me,"
said Red Riding Hood.

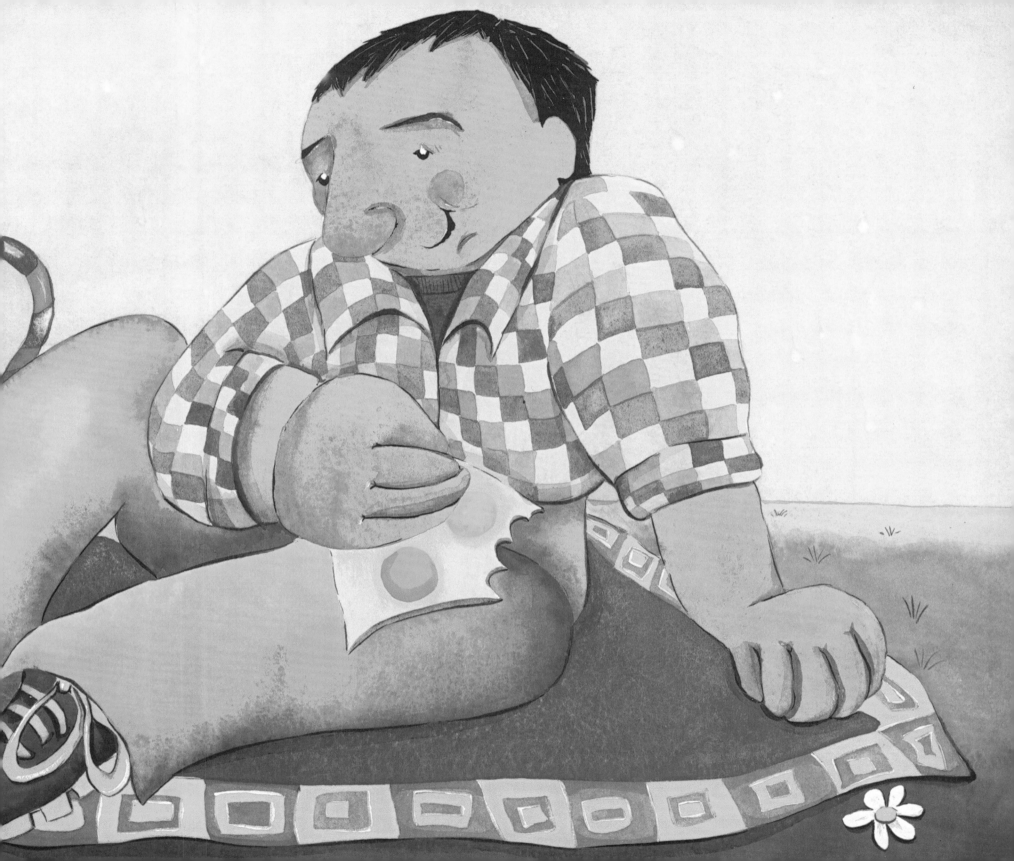

وانتهت جميع الكوكيز.

And then there were none.